"What if Buzzard has Rabbit and his family trapped somewhere?" asked Shrew.

Mole nodded. "You're right. We have to go to the police ourselves."

"No," said Shrew. "One of us has to go to the police. The other one has to keep watch at Buzzard's house."

Mole shivered. "Which one?"

"The braver one," said Shrew.

"Phew," said Mole. "Thank you for volunteering, Shrew."

Shrew rolled her eyes.

Books by Jackie French Koller

Picture Books

Bouncing on the Bed

Nickommoh! A Thanksgiving Celebration

No Such Thing

One Monkey Too Many

Chapter Books

The *Dragonling* books

The *Mole and Shrew* series

The Promise

Novels: Middle-Grade & Up

If I Had One Wish . . .

The Last Voyage of the Misty Day

Nothing to Fear

The Primrose Way

Novels: Young Adult

The Falcon

A Place to Call Home

Mole AND Shrew
Find a Clue

by Jackie French Koller
illustrated by Anne Reas

A STEPPING STONE BOOK™
Random House 🏠 New York

To Chuck, world's greatest brother-in-law

Text copyright © 2001 by Jackie French Koller
Illustrations copyright © 2001 by Anne Reas

www.randomhouse.com/kids

Library of Congress Cataloging-in-Publication Data
Koller, Jackie French.
Mole and Shrew find a clue / by Jackie French Koller ; illustrated by Anne Reas.
p.   cm.   "A stepping stone book."
Summary: When Mole overhears Buzzard's idea to have Rabbit and his family
for dinner, Mole and his friend Shrew set out to warn Rabbit.
ISBN 0-375-80692-X (trade) — ISBN 0-375-90692-4 (lib. bdg.)
[1. Moles (Animals)—Fiction. 2. Shrews—Fiction. 3. Animals—Fiction.]
I. Reas, Anne, ill.   II. Title.
PZ7.K833 Mon   2001   [Fic]—dc21   00-067325

Printed in the United States of America   October 2001   10 9 8 7 6 5 4 3 2 1

☀ Contents ☀

❊ 1 *❊*

Rabbit Stew

Mole wandered down the cookie row of Badger's Market. Suddenly, BUMP! Someone nearly bowled him over!

Mole turned to see Buzzard blinking at him in surprise.

"Heavens!" said Mole. "What is your hurry?"

"I'm sorry," said Buzzard. "I didn't see you there. I'm just a bit excited. I'm having a big dinner tonight!"

Mole shook his head as Buzzard dashed

away. "It's a mystery to me how anyone could get *that* excited about food," he muttered. "No wonder Buzzard is so plump."

Mole turned back to the cookies.

"Now, where was I?" he mumbled. "Oh yes. Cookies. Hmmm. What kind should I pick? Chocolate chips are nice, but oh! So are vanilla creams. Yes, I think it will be vanilla creams. Or, mmmm, peanut butter patties. . . ." Mole licked his lips. "Such a hard choice." Mole reached the end of the row. "Fig bars!" he cried. "Just the thing." He tucked a package under his arm and started for the checkout.

On his way through the vegetable section, Mole noticed Buzzard speaking with Badger.

"You're having Rabbit and his family

for dinner?" Mole heard Badger ask.

Mole's mouth fell open. He stopped in his tracks.

"Yes," Buzzard replied. "Tonight. I'll need some carrots and potatoes and onions. I plan to make a stew, you see."

Mole shivered. So *this* was the big dinner Buzzard was so excited about. Rabbit stew!

"I didn't know you were fond of Rabbit," said Badger.

"Oh yes," said Buzzard. "Very fond. I'll be making quite a lot of stew, so make sure you give me plenty of vegetables."

"Did you notice that I'm having a sale on stew bowls?" said Badger.

"Thank you anyway," said Buzzard, "but I always serve Rabbit on my finest china."

Mole had heard enough.

"What kind of a beast are you?" he yelled at Buzzard. Buzzard squinted at Mole.

"I beg your pardon?" she said.

"How dare you have Rabbit for dinner!" said Mole. "Rabbit is my friend."

"Well then, I'll have *you* for dinner, too," said Buzzard. "I've plenty of room."

Mole's eyes dropped to Buzzard's large belly.

"That's a terrific idea," said Badger. "I'll throw in a couple more potatoes."

Mole looked at Badger, horrified.

"How can you be so heartless?" he cried. Then he dropped his package of cookies and rushed for the door.

"I have to warn Rabbit!" Mole said to himself as he scurried down Main Street.

The shortest road to Hidden Hollow,

where Mole and Rabbit lived, was Bittersweet Lane. But Gnarly Knoll, where Buzzard lived, was *on* Bittersweet Lane. Mole didn't want to go *anywhere* near Buzzard's house.

PLOP! A raindrop landed on Mole's nose.

"Oh dear," said Mole. "It's almost dark and now it's starting to rain."

There was no time to waste. Mole turned onto Bittersweet Lane.

"I'll go very fast," he said. "I'll be safe in Hidden Hollow before Buzzard returns home to Gnarly Knoll."

A brisk wind had come up. Dry leaves scurried across Mole's path. More raindrops began to plop all around him.

As he neared Gnarly Knoll, Mole shivered. He had always thought Buzzard's old mansion was spooky-looking. Now, as he

stared at the tall turrets and dark stone walls, goose bumps popped out all over him.

How many poor creatures had met their fate in Buzzard's stewpot? Mole wondered.

"Oww . . . ," came a cry.

Mole nearly jumped out of his skin. Was he hearing things? Was someone in trouble? Or was it just the wind thrashing in the nearby trees?

In the distance, thunder rumbled.

"Yeowww!" came another cry from the direction of Gnarly Knoll.

Mole swallowed hard. Someone *was* in trouble! Could it be Rabbit? Was Buzzard's cook . . . ? Mole couldn't bear to think of it!

"Who . . . who's there?" he called.

No one answered.

"Perhaps it *was* just the wind," Mole told himself.

Dark clouds boiled in the sky. A bright streak of lightning flashed and the thunder grew louder.

"Help!" someone screamed.

"Oh dear," mumbled Mole. He bit his lip and stared at Gnarly Knoll.

"Mole!" a voice suddenly shouted.

Mole turned.

It was Buzzard, hurrying toward him through the dark!

* 2 *

Run, Mole, Run!

"Aagh!" cried Mole. He started to run.

"Wait!" cried Buzzard. "I've been trying to catch you."

"Aagh!" cried Mole again. He ran faster.

Raindrops pelted down. Trees began tossing their branches about. They looked like angry monsters, grabbing at Mole with bony arms.

KA-BOOM! Lightning streaked across the sky and struck a nearby tree. A huge branch crashed to the ground, barely missing Mole!

"Oh my!" cried Mole.

More streaks of lightning zigzagged around him. Hailstones stung his back like angry bees. Before long, his clothes were drenched.

Mole ran and ran until he reached Hidden Hollow. His whole neighborhood was in darkness! The storm must have knocked the power out. Mole ran right past his own house, up to his friend Shrew's door.

"Shrew!" he cried, pounding wildly. "Shrew, open up!"

Shrew pulled her door open and a great gust of wind pushed Mole inside. He was huffing and puffing, and dripping all over the rug.

"Heavens!" cried Shrew. "What are you doing out in this storm, Mole?"

"Something terrible is about to happen," Mole gasped. "In fact, it may even be happening already!"

Shrew peered out her door.

"Where?" she asked.

"Not out there," said Mole. "Up at Gnarly Knoll!"

Shrew's eyes grew wide. "Buzzard's place?" she said.

Mole nodded.

"Are you sure?" asked Shrew.

"Quite sure," said Mole. "I heard someone scream for help."

"And you didn't stop?" asked Shrew.

"I was going to," said Mole. "But then Buzzard shouted and came after me! I got scared and ran."

"How strange," said Shrew. "Perhaps we should call the police."

Shrew picked up her phone.

"Hello? Hello?" she said. She jiggled the
receiver.

12

"What's wrong?" asked Mole.

"The phone seems to be dead," said Shrew.

"Oh," said Mole. "The poor thing. Do you think we should have a funeral?"

Shrew looked puzzled. "A funeral?" she said.

"Yes," said Mole, "for the phone."

Shrew laughed and shook her head. "No, no! The phone isn't *dead* dead, Mole. It just isn't working—probably because of the storm."

"Well, that's a very different story," said Mole. "You should be careful who you call *dead*, Shrew. There are lots of times when *I'm* not working. I wouldn't want to be buried by mistake."

Shrew giggled and nodded. "I will try to be more careful, Mole," she said.

"So what do we do now?" asked Mole.

"We'll have to go ourselves," said Shrew.

"To the police?"

"No," said Shrew. "Whoever you heard scream may be hurt. It could be too late by the time we get to town and back. We have to go to Gnarly Knoll ourselves."

Mole swallowed hard. "But . . . what about Buzzard?" he said.

"What *about* Buzzard?" asked Shrew.

"She might eat us," said Mole.

"Eat us?" cried Shrew.

"Yes." Mole lowered his voice as if he were afraid someone might be listening. "You see," he whispered, "I overheard Buzzard and Badger talking at the grocery store. Buzzard said she was planning to *eat* Rabbit! Then she said she wanted to eat me, too!"

3

To the Rescue!

Shrew stared at Mole. "Have you lost your mind?" she asked.

"I don't think so," said Mole. He felt his head. "Why? Does my head look empty?"

Shrew shook her head. "No, Mole," she said. "Although sometimes I wonder. . . ."

"Sometimes I wonder, too," said Mole. "I wonder why a tree's bark is silent and why fish don't have feet. I wonder why it's not my birthday every day. I wonder . . ."

"*Mole*," said Shrew. "That's all very

interesting, but what *I'm* wondering is, what exactly did you hear Buzzard say?"

"She said she was going to put Rabbit and his family in a stew," said Mole.

"What?" cried Shrew. "She told you that?"

"She told Badger," said Mole, "while I was standing there."

Shrew shook her head in disbelief. "What did you say?" she asked.

"I told her she couldn't do that," said Mole.

"And what did *she* say?" asked Shrew.

"She said she was going to eat *me*, too!"

Shrew's eyes bulged. "I can't believe it. I'm sure there must be some mistake," she said.

"Then who was screaming at Gnarly Knoll?" asked Mole.

Shrew chewed her lip. "I forgot about that," she said. "We'd better go find out."

"But the storm," said Mole.

"Storm or no storm," said Shrew. "If someone is in trouble, we have to go."

Mole took a deep breath. If Shrew could be brave, he could be, too.

"I'll go home and get my rain gear," he said.

"Hurry," said Shrew. "I'll meet you by your front gate in five minutes."

Mole rushed out into a wall of icy cold rain. Lightning flashed and thunder rumbled. He dashed across Shrew's front yard to his house. He pushed through the door and stood panting in the hall.

Mole's house was dark, but it was cozy and dry. It felt very safe.

Perhaps I should tell Shrew I feel feverish,

he thought. But he felt guilty.

No, Mole, he told himself. *Shrew is counting on you, and someone else may need you—someone who is about to be put in a stew!*

Mole opened his front closet and felt along the top shelf for his flashlight. He got it down and flicked the switch.

Nothing.

"Drat," said Mole. He tried again, but the light wouldn't go on. "I wish I had some extra batteries," he said. "I hope Shrew has a flashlight that works."

Mole put on his red slicker, rain hat, and green plastic boots. He rushed back out into the storm.

Shrew was waiting by the gate with a small flashlight. Its beam was barely visible.

"Is that the only flashlight you have?" asked Mole.

"Yes," said Shrew. "I was hoping you had a bigger one."

"I do," said Mole, "but it is out of batteries. Perhaps I should go back and get a lantern."

"It will only blow out in this wind," said Shrew. "If we stay together, we'll be fine."

CRR-ACKLE! KA-BOOM!

Mole and Shrew jumped as lightning flashed and thunder struck.

CRR-ACK! CRR-RUMPH!

A great tree crashed down across the path. Broken branches scattered in all directions.

"That was close," said Shrew. "This is the worst storm I can remember!"

"Me too," said Mole. "Maybe we should wait until it's over."

"That could be hours," said Shrew. "It might be too late for whoever needs our help."

"But that tree has blocked the path," said Mole.

"Don't worry," said Shrew. "Just follow me. I have a very good sense of direction."

Shrew stepped off the path into the deep woods. Mole followed.

Mole and Shrew walked and walked.

"Shrew," said Mole, "shouldn't we have found the path again by now?"

"I'm sure it's just ahead," said Shrew.

Rain dripped from Mole's rain hat. The wind tore at his slicker. Lightning crackled around him and the muddy ground squished beneath his boots.

"What was that?" Mole asked suddenly.

"What was what?" asked Shrew.

"I heard something moan."

"I didn't hear anything," said Shrew. "I'm sure it was just a tree creaking in the wind."

"It didn't sound like a tree," said Mole. His hair was standing on end.

"Just keep walking," said Shrew. "The path has to be very close."

Suddenly, Mole felt something grab him around the ankle.

"Aagh!" he shrieked. "Aagh! She's got me! Buzzard's got me!"

Shrew hurried back. She looked at Mole's foot.

"It's a tree root, Mole," she said. "You've snagged your foot in a tree root."

"Oh," said Mole. He untangled his foot and followed Shrew quietly.

Then something grabbed his slicker and held it tight!

"Aagh!" shrieked Mole. "She's got me now! She's got my coat!"

Shrew hurried back again. She looked over Mole's shoulder.

"It's a bramble, Mole," she said. "You're hooked on a bramble."

"Oh," said Mole. He freed his coat and followed Shrew sheepishly.

"Shrew!" he yelled suddenly.

Shrew stopped and turned around.

"What *now*, Mole?" she asked.

"I see a house!" said Mole. "Look!" He pointed through the woods.

Shrew peered through the dark and the rain.

"Why, I believe you're right, Mole," she said. "It is a house. It's . . . it's . . ." Then she groaned. "It's *your* house, Mole. We've been walking in circles!"

4

Gnarly Knoll

"We're going *over* the tree this time," said Shrew. "I'm not letting this path out of my sight."

Huffing and puffing, Mole and Shrew scrambled over the huge tree. They jumped down on the other side and started off along the lane.

"Please try and be brave, Mole," said Shrew. "We have no time to waste."

The storm still crashed around them. Trees leaned over and battered Mole with their branches. Leaves blew through the air. They plastered themselves to Mole's face and to his slicker. Rain dripped down and trickled into his boots.

Squish, squish, squish went Mole as he trudged bravely on.

At last a flash of lightning lit up the night and there stood Gnarly Knoll, outlined against the sky.

Mole shivered. "Why would anyone want to live in a creepy old place like that?" he asked.

Shrew shrugged. "Buzzard always has been an odd duck," she said.

"She has?" said Mole. "Then why is she called Buzzard?"

"Because she *is* a buzzard," said Shrew.

"Is a buzzard a kind of duck?" asked Mole.

"No, Mole," said Shrew. "It's just an expression."

"What's just an expression?" asked Mole.

"*Odd duck,*" said Shrew.

Mole scratched his head. "That *is* odd," he said. "I know a lot of expressions, like smiles and frowns. What kind of expression is an odd duck, Shrew? If someone has an odd duck on their face, are they happy or sad?"

Shrew started to laugh. "Well, if I had an odd duck on my face, I don't think *I'd* be too happy," she said.

"It's a sad expression, then?" asked Mole.

"No. It's not that kind of expression at all," said Shrew. She sighed. "It's just a saying. It means that Buzzard is a bit unusual. And because she's so unusual, I think that Gnarly Knoll suits her very well."

"Well, it doesn't suit me," said Mole. "The sooner we're done with this business, the better."

They reached the old iron gates of Gnarly Knoll. Shrew pushed them open.

CRR-EE-EAK . . .

"Shush!" whispered Mole. "We don't want Buzzard to hear us!"

"Why?" asked Shrew.

"What if she's up to no good?" said Mole. "What if she catches us spying and puts us in her stew?"

"Mole," said Shrew, "I still think you're all wet."

"Well, of course I'm all wet!" said Mole. "It's pouring rain!"

Shrew chuckled. "*All wet* is another expression," she said. "It means I think you are mistaken."

"In that case," said Mole, "I think *you're* all wet. And I know another old expression. *It's better to be safe than sorry.*"

"All right," said Shrew. "We'll poke around the outside of the house first and see what we can see."

"Shut off that flashlight," said Mole. "We don't want Buzzard to see us."

Shrew turned off the light.

Mole and Shrew crept up Gnarly Knoll's long, twisting driveway. When they got close, they saw candlelight flickering through a window at the back of the house. They made their way quietly around to a small covered porch by the back door.

"Shush," said Mole. "I hear someone talking."

5

Secret Ingredients

Mole and Shrew stood still and listened. They could hear muffled voices coming from inside.

"What are they saying?" asked Mole.

"I can't hear," said Shrew. "Let's go closer to the window."

They bent low and crept over to the window.

"It's too high for me. Can you see?" asked Shrew.

Mole stretched up on tippy-toes.

"No, it's too high for me, too. Why don't you climb up on my shoulders, Shrew?"

Shrew shook her head. "I'm afraid I can't," she said. "Heights give me nose-bleeds."

"Perhaps I should climb up on your shoulders, then," said Mole.

Shrew stared up at Mole. "Um . . . I don't mean to be impolite, Mole," she said, "but have you noticed how much, um . . . *larger* you are than I am?"

Mole looked down at Shrew. "You're right, Shrew," he said. "You're far too puny for standing on."

"Maybe you can just listen," said Shrew.

Mole stretched up on tippy-toes again.

"Yes," he whispered. "I can hear now. I hear pots and pans. This must be the kitchen window. And I hear Buzzard

talking with someone. I believe it's Crow, her cook."

"What are they saying?" asked Shrew.

Mole listened closely.

"Did you get the vegetables?" Crow was asking.

"Yes," Buzzard answered. "Did you get the rest of the ingredients?"

"All except for your *secret ingredients*," said Crow. "I only got one before the storm hit."

"I'll get the rest," said Buzzard. "It's dirty work anyway. I don't expect you to do it."

Mole shivered.

"Buzzard is talking about capturing the rabbits," he whispered to Shrew.

"When will you go after them?" asked Crow.

"As soon as the storm lets up a little,"

said Buzzard. "It will be too muddy otherwise and I'll have a hard time grabbing them. The little ones are the worst. They're so slippery and they cling so tight to the ground. Sometimes I end up popping their little heads right off!"

"Oh," gasped Mole.

"What is it?" whispered Shrew.

"It's awful," said Mole. "She's talking about the children! Hush! They're saying something else."

"What if the storm doesn't let up?" Crow was asking. "Can you do without the little ones?"

"But the little ones are so sweet and tender," said Buzzard. "They're my very favorite. I'm sure the storm can't last much longer. If I have to, I can always use a knife."

Mole shuddered.

"Well, just make sure you leave a few for next time," said Crow.

"Don't worry," said Buzzard. "New babies are always popping up. There'll be plenty more the next time we're in the mood for a stew."

"Aagh!" whispered Mole. He crouched down. "I've heard enough!" he said to Shrew. "We've got to save Rabbit. Buzzard is going after him as soon as the storm lets up!"

"Are you sure?" asked Shrew, wide-eyed.

"Yes," whispered Mole. "It's terrible, Shrew. She said that the children are her favorite because they're so sweet and tender." Mole shuddered again. "She said they cling to the ground so tight. When she's trying to grab them, sometimes she pops their little heads off!"

Shrew put a hand to her mouth. "How awful!" she gasped.

Mole suddenly pointed to the floor of the porch.

"What's that?" he whispered.

In the light of the window, he could see a trail of dark spots leading up to the back door.

Shrew bent down and touched a finger to one of the spots. Then she brought her finger to her nose. She stood and stared at Mole with wide eyes.

"It's . . . *blood*," she said.

❊6❊

Carried Away

"I know a shortcut to Rabbit's house," said Shrew. "We can cut through Bayberry Meadow."

"Do you think it's wise to be out in a meadow in a lightning storm?" asked Mole.

"Mole," said Shrew, "it is not wise to be *out* in a lightning storm—period. But this is an emergency."

"Good point," said Mole.

He followed Shrew through Buzzard's

backyard and into the meadow.

CRRACKLE, CRRACK! KA-BOOM!

Mole ducked and jumped as lightning crinkled and thunder crashed.

"I hope we make it through this night in one piece," said Mole.

SPLASH!

"What was *that*?" asked Mole.

Shrew didn't answer, and her light was gone!

Mole peered into the darkness. He couldn't see anything.

"Shrew?" he cried.

Still no answer.

"Shrew!" Mole called loudly.

"*Mrrruffle merp glug!*" someone replied.

"Shrew?" called Mole. "Is that you?"

"Yes—*blurble*—yes!" gasped Shrew. Her voice was growing more and more distant.

"Shrew, where are you?" cried Mole. "What's happened?"

"The brook," cried Shrew. "It's—*blurp, gurgle*—swollen out of its banks! Help!"

"Oh my goodness!" cried Mole. "Shrew has gotten carried away!"

He stumbled through the darkness until . . .

SPLASH!

Mole tumbled into the brook, too!

Cold water rushed over him. It seeped into his coat. It filled up his boots.

"Helrp—*gurgle*—helrp!" cried Shrew. "I'm holding on . . . *glub* . . . The current is too strong, and I'm too small. I can't—*gasp*—fight it!"

"I'm coming!" cried Mole. "I'm coming, Shrew."

Mole tried to swim, but his heavy boots dragged him down.

"Oh my," he said to himself. "Now what do I do?"

"Mole—*blurple, gurgle, blup*—where are you?" hollered Shrew.

"I can't swim!" cried Mole.

"*Ach! Gasp! Gurgle!* Of course you can," cried Shrew. "You go swimming all the—*glurp*—time!"

"Not with boots on!" shouted Mole.

"Well—*gasp*—take your boots off!"

"In this storm?" cried Mole. "I might catch cold!"

"*Mole!*" shrieked Shrew. "I'm—*glubble, gasp—drowning!*"

"Oh dear!" Mole reached down and tugged off his boots. He struck off through the water.

When Mole reached Shrew, she was clinging to a branch of a fallen tree.

"Oh, Mole," she cried. "Thank heaven!"

Mole climbed up on a rock. He looked at the sky. "Thank you!" he called.

"What—*glub*—are you doing?" cried Shrew.

"Thanking heaven," said Mole.

"Mole!" shrieked Shrew. *"Save me first!"*

Mole sighed. "I wish you'd make up your mind what you want," he said.

☀ 7 ☀

Trespassers Two

Mole was tired, wet, and footsore by the time he and Shrew reached Rabbit's house. Shrew was soaked through and shivering. And the flashlight was gone, lost in the raging brook.

"I do hope you're right about all this, Mole," said Shrew.

Mole knocked on Rabbit's door.

"I *am* right," said Mole. "Just wait till you see how grateful Rabbit is when we save him and his family."

They waited and waited. Nobody came to the door.

"Perhaps they're sleeping," said Shrew. "Knock louder."

Mole knocked again.

Still no answer.

"Oh dear," said Mole. "You don't think . . . you don't think Buzzard got here first, do you?"

"I hope not," said Shrew. She pressed her face against Rabbit's window. "I don't see anyone," she said. "Perhaps we had better go in and have a look around."

"But that's trespassing," said Mole. "Trespassing is against the law."

"So is putting people in a stew," said Shrew. "Would you rather have someone trespass on your property or put you in a stew?"

"Good point," said Mole. He turned the doorknob.

Mole and Shrew stepped inside. It felt good to be out of the storm at last.

"Hello," called Mole.

"Anyone home?" cried Shrew.

No answer.

A flash of lightning lit up the room for a second. Mole saw a candle and a book of matches on a small table by the door. Then it was dark again. He felt around on the table until he found the matches. He lit the candle.

The candle made a small circle of light.

Mole and Shrew looked around. They were in the living room. More lightning flashed outside. It cast strange shadows on the walls.

"What's that?" cried Mole.

"What?" asked Shrew.

"Aagh!" screamed Mole. "It's a head!!!" He dropped the candle and nearly bowled Shrew over on his way out the door.

"Mole!" Shrew called after him. "Mole!"

Mole looked back over his shoulder. A flash of lightning lit up Shrew. She was standing in the doorway, holding the head in her hands!

"Shrew! How could you?" Mole shrieked.

"Mole," Shrew shouted, "calm down! It's not a *head*. It's just a ball."

Mole stopped running. "Oh," he said. He turned around and walked back to Rabbit's house.

"Mole," said Shrew, "you dropped the candle and nearly set the carpet on fire."

"I'm terribly sorry," said Mole. "It's just that . . . when I saw that round thing, I sort of panicked."

"I know," said Shrew. "I'll tell you what. Let's make a pact."

"A pack of what?" Mole asked.

"Not a pack, Mole, a pact. A pact is an agreement. Let's agree not to cry out about something until we're quite sure what it is."

"Good idea," said Mole.

"Now follow me," said Shrew.

"Where?" asked Mole.

"Back into the house," said Shrew.

"But . . . ," said Mole. "But there could be *bodies* in there!"

"Mole," said Shrew, "may I remind you that this whole mission was your idea. I am cold. I am wet. I nearly drowned tonight. If you don't get in here and help me get to the bottom of this, there may very well be a body out *there*!"

Mole gasped. "Where?"

Shrew sighed. "Never mind, Mole. Just get in here."

Footsteps in the Dark

"There isn't anyone here," said Shrew, "and there is no sign of a struggle."

Mole scratched his head. "They must be hiding out," he said. "Crow already got one of them, don't forget. Maybe they went to the police."

"Of course!" said Shrew. "How foolish we are. They aren't going to be sitting here waiting for Buzzard to strike again."

Mole let out a sigh of relief.

"So we can go home, then," he said.

Shrew considered. "I'm afraid not, Mole," she said. "We just can't be sure. What if Buzzard has Rabbit and his family trapped somewhere?"

Mole nodded. "You're right, Shrew. We have to go to the police ourselves."

"No," said Shrew. "One of us has to go to the police. The other one has to keep watch at Buzzard's house."

Mole shivered. "Which one?"

"The braver one," said Shrew.

"Phew," said Mole. "Thank you for volunteering, Shrew."

Shrew rolled her eyes.

Mole and Shrew grew quiet as they got close to Gnarly Knoll. The storm had stopped at last and the dark clouds were clearing.

SLAM!

Mole jumped. "What was *that*?" he asked.

"Sounded like a door," said Shrew. "Quick. Hide!"

Mole and Shrew dove into the bushes. Soon they heard footsteps approaching.

"It's Buzzard," whispered Shrew, "and she's carrying a basket."

"And a knife!" Mole added hoarsely.

"She's going after them!" said Shrew.

"What do we do?" asked Mole.

"We follow her," said Shrew.

Mole swallowed hard.

"But . . . she has a knife," he said. "A butcher knife!"

Shrew nodded. "You're right," she said. "We'll need help. I'll follow her. You run to the police."

"But how will I find you?" asked Mole.

"I'll leave a trail," said Shrew. "Like

this." She snapped a branch. "Just follow the trail of broken branches."

"All right," said Mole.

Shrew set off after Buzzard.

"Shrew," called Mole, "be careful!"

A Tough Case

Mole ran into the police station. Sergeant Squirrel was busily writing at her desk.

"Excuse me," said Mole.

Squirrel looked up.

"I'll be with you in a moment," she said.

"But this is important," said Mole.

"This is important, too," said Squirrel. "I have a very tough case and I can't seem to crack it."

"Try a sledgehammer," said Mole.

"A what?" asked Squirrel.

"A sledgehammer," Mole repeated. "I've found you can crack almost anything with a sledgehammer—even rocks."

Squirrel stared at Mole.

"Thank you," she said. "I'll remember that, next time I want to crack a *rock*. Now, how can I help you?"

"There's going to be a murder," said Mole.

Squirrel's ears perked up.

"A murder?" she said. "How do you know?"

"I heard Badger and Buzzard talking about it," said Mole.

Squirrel frowned. "Badger and Buzzard are very upstanding citizens," she said.

"What does the way they stand have to do with anything?" asked Mole.

Squirrel looked confused. "Never

mind," she said. "Go on, please. Tell me exactly what you heard."

"I heard Buzzard telling Badger that she wanted to eat Rabbit and his family for dinner," said Mole.

Sergeant Squirrel stroked her chin. "Are you sure you heard right?" she asked.

"Yes," said Mole. "When I spoke up, Buzzard threatened to eat *me*, too."

"Doesn't sound like Buzzard," said Squirrel. "But maybe we ought to put a tail on her, just to be safe."

"Oh, she already has a tail," said Mole.

Squirrel frowned. "Well, if you've already put a tail on her, what do you expect me to do?" she asked.

"*I* didn't put the tail on her," said Mole.

"Well, who did, then?" asked Squirrel.

"How should I know? Her mother, I suppose," said Mole.

"Her mother put a tail on her?" asked Squirrel.

"Well, in a manner of speaking," said Mole. "I suppose her father had something to do with it, too."

Squirrel scratched her head. "Mole," she said, "somehow I don't think we're talking about the same thing. Perhaps we had better start over, from the beginning."

☀10☀

On the Trail

Shrew's trail led down Bittersweet Lane away from Gnarly Knoll. It went in to Bayberry Meadow.

"I knew it!" cried Mole. "This is the shortcut to Rabbit's house!"

Squirrel shined her flashlight into the meadow. "And you say Buzzard had a knife?" she asked.

"A *butcher* knife!" said Mole.

"Let's go," said Squirrel.

Mole led the way. He was careful to

steer clear of the brook this time. When they reached Rabbit's house, Squirrel switched off the light. She and Mole hid behind the hedge.

"Looks pretty quiet," said Squirrel.

Mole gulped. "Maybe Buzzard has come and gone," he said. "Maybe it's all over. I hope Shrew is safe!"

Squirrel turned her flashlight back on and looked around. "What's that?" she asked.

"What?" asked Mole.

"Isn't that another broken branch?" said Squirrel. "It looks to me like the trail keeps going."

"So it does," said Mole. "How odd. Unless . . ."

"Unless what?" asked Squirrel.

"Unless Rabbit and his family heard Buzzard coming and ran away. Maybe

59

Buzzard followed them. And maybe Shrew followed Buzzard."

"Good thinking," said Squirrel. "Press on."

Mole and Squirrel followed the trail into the woods and down to Skunk Cabbage Swamp.

"Look!" cried Mole. "The ground is all dug up!"

"So it is," said Squirrel. "Must have been a struggle."

"Dear me," said Mole. "I do hope Shrew is okay."

"Judging from this, I'd say she is," said Squirrel. She pointed to yet another broken branch. "She's *still* leaving a trail."

"Let's go," said Mole.

Shrew's trail went on and on. It wound through the swamp, across Gooseberry Glen, down Huckleberry Hill, and right up to Gnarly Knoll's back door!

"Look!" cried Mole. He pointed to a little yellow mound on the porch floor. "That's Shrew's rain hat! Buzzard has got Shrew!"

"All right," said Squirrel. "Here's the plan. You stand out here and make a ruckus. I'll hide beside the door, and when Buzzard comes out, I'll nab her."

"What's a 'ruckus'?" asked Mole.

"It's a lot of noise," said Squirrel.

"I'm not sure I know how to make a lot of noise," said Mole.

"Use your imagination," said Squirrel.

"All right," said Mole. He closed his eyes and stood very still.

"What are you doing?" asked Squirrel.

"I'm using my imagination," said Mole. "Can you hear me?"

Squirrel rolled her eyes and shook her

head. "Just shout, Mole," she said. "Shout and holler and jump up and down."

"What should I shout?" asked Mole.

"Anything you like," said Squirrel.

Mole started jumping up and down. "Christmas, birthday cake, apple pie!" he yelled. "Books, flowers, chocolate chip cookies!"

"What on earth are you shouting?" asked Squirrel.

"I'm shouting things I like," said Mole. "Isn't that what you said?"

"Yes, I guess it is," said Squirrel, "but . . ."

Suddenly, Buzzard's door opened.

Squirrel flattened herself against the wall.

Mole trembled.

☀11☀

Just in Time!

"Mole!" cried Buzzard. "I thought I heard someone out here. I'm so glad it's you. I've been trying to catch you. Wait right here."

Squirrel dove off the porch into a bush.

Buzzard turned around and disappeared into the house again.

"She's going to get the knife!" whispered Mole.

"Good," said Squirrel. "Then we'll catch her red-handed."

"What difference does it make what

color her hands are?" asked Mole.

"Shush," said Squirrel. "Here she comes."

Out walked Buzzard.

Mole closed his eyes.

"Here, Mole," said Buzzard. "I've been trying to give you this."

Mole cringed and closed his eyes, afraid to feel the prick of Buzzard's knife.

Nothing happened.

Mole opened one eye. He looked at what Buzzard held in her hand.

"Fig bars?" he said.

"Yes," said Buzzard. "You dropped them at the market. I was trying to catch you to give them back."

"Um," said Mole, "well, that's very kind, but—"

"It has worked out perfectly that you came now," Buzzard interrupted. "You're just in time for the stew."

"Oh, no you don't!" said Mole, backing up. "Nab her, Sergeant. Nab her quick!"

Squirrel jumped out of the bush.

Buzzard turned around.

"Sergeant Squirrel!" she said. "What are you doing here?"

Squirrel cleared her throat. "Well," she said, "Mole has a notion that you are planning to eat Rabbit."

"Eat Rabbit!" Buzzard's eyes popped. She turned to Mole. "Where on earth did you get such an idea?" she asked.

"At the market," said Mole. "I heard you say so to Badger."

Buzzard scratched her head for a moment. Then she tipped her head back and laughed. "I think you're confused, Mole," she said. "Please come inside. You too, Squirrel."

Squirrel started after Buzzard.

"Be careful," Mole whispered. "It might be a trap."

"Don't worry," said Squirrel. "I'm keeping my eyes open."

"Well, I should hope so," whispered Mole. "Otherwise, you'd just be walking around bumping into things."

Squirrel sighed. "Never mind, Mole," she said. "Just stay close behind me, please."

Buzzard led Squirrel and Mole through her kitchen. Then she pushed open the door to her dining room. There, seated around the candlelit table, were Rabbit and all his family—and Shrew!

"Mole!" cried Shrew. "I'm so glad you made it. I didn't know if I'd marked the trail well enough."

"See?" said Buzzard. "When I said I was

67

having Rabbit for dinner, I meant as a *guest*, not as the main course."

Squirrel sniffed. "I suspected something like this all along," she said.

Mole folded his arms over his chest.

"Not so fast, Buzzard," he said. "Why don't you tell the sergeant about your *secret ingredients*?"

"The mushrooms?" asked Buzzard.

"Mushrooms?" repeated Mole.

"Yes," said Buzzard. "I pick them down at Skunk Cabbage Swamp. It's a messy business, but it's worth it. They're *so* tasty. The little ones are the best. They're so tender and sweet!"

Mole looked at Shrew.

"It's true, Mole," said Shrew. "I helped her gather them myself."

Mole thought and thought. Something still didn't add up.

"Wait a minute!" he cried. "Who was yelling for help, then? And what about the blood on the back porch?"

Crow came in with a steaming bowl of stew in her hands.

"That was me, I'm afraid," she said. "I went out to pick the mushrooms earlier. But then the storm started. In my rush to get back, I ran right into a briar patch. Thank goodness Buzzard came along and plucked me out. My poor legs got scratched to ribbons, though."

Crow put the bowl on the table. She lifted her skirt to her knees. Her legs were covered with bandages.

Mole's ears started to burn. He looked down at his feet. "Um . . . I'm afraid I owe you an apology, Buzzard," he mumbled.

Buzzard came over and patted Mole on the back. "No harm done, Mole," she said.

71

"It was all just a big misunderstanding. Won't you and Squirrel stay for dinner? I have plenty of vegetable stew. *And* I made a yummy surprise for dessert."

Mole licked his lips. "I *am* hungry," he said. "And I *am* very fond of dessert. What is your yummy surprise, Buzzard?"

"Chocolate mousse," said Buzzard.

Mole's eyes bugged out. "Chocolate *moose*!" he croaked.

Want to spend more time with
MOle AND Shrew?

Find out how Mole
and Shrew met in:

Spend a funny year with
Mole and Shrew in:

Join Mole and Shrew as they
look for the perfect job in:

Jackie French Koller

is the mother of three grown children, the wife of a wonderful man named George, and the author of over two dozen books for children and young adults. She lives on a mountaintop in western Massachusetts, where she shares her studio with her doll, Susie; her dogs, Sara and Cassie; hundreds of books; a cranky computer; piles of papers; assorted dust bunnies; and all of the creatures of her imagination, including her old and dear friends Mole and Shrew.